Did you pack the can opener?

Psst—I think I just heard something....

For Jacqui

First U.S. edition 2010

Library of Congress Cataloging-in-Publication Data

Schwarz, Viviane.
There are no cats in this book / Viviane Schwarz.
—1st U.S. ed.
p. cm.
Summary: Filled with the spirit of adventure,
three cats pack their suitcases and try
to escape from their book.
ISBN 978-0-7636-4954-8
1. Toy and movable books. [1. Cats—Fiction.
2. Humorous stories. 3. Toy and movable books.]
I. Title.
PZ7.S41145Ti 2010
(E)—dc22   2009051510

10 11 12 13 14 15 16 TWPS 10 9 8 7 6 5 4 3 2 1

Printed in Malaysia

This book was typeset in Kingthings Trypewriter.
The illustrations were done in brush and ink.

Candlewick Press
99 Dover Street
Somerville, Massachusetts 02144

visit us at www.candlewick.com

CANDLEWICK PRESS

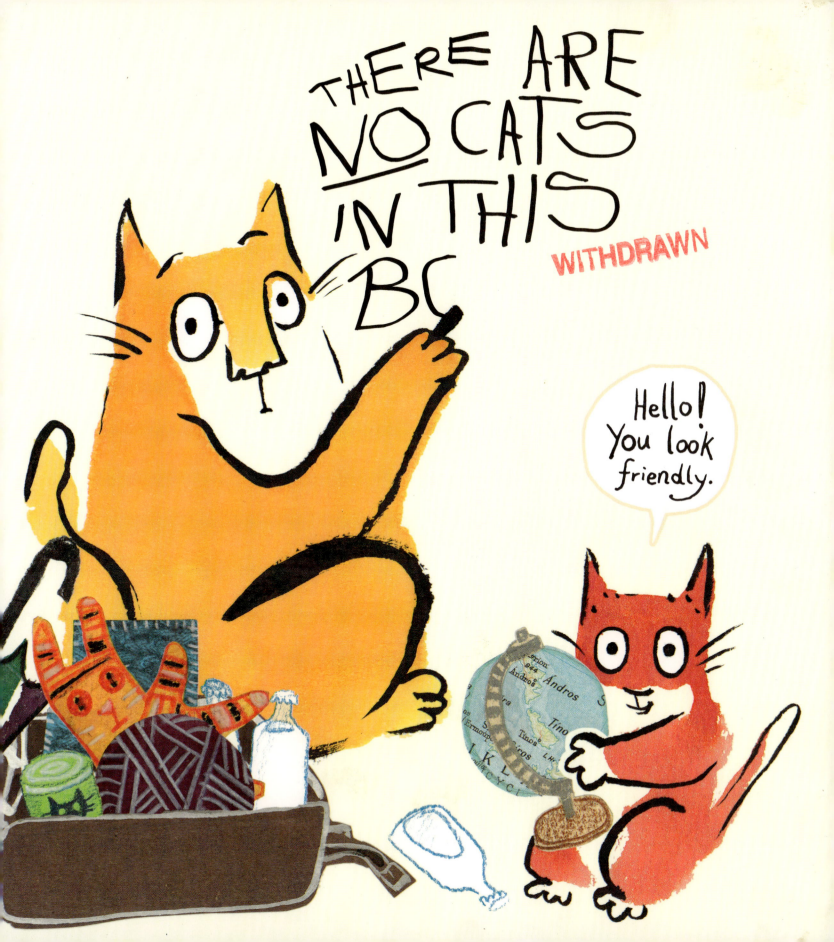

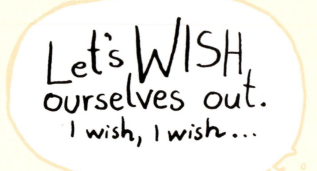

I wish, I wish, I wish, I wish, I wish, I wish, I wish, I wish, I wish, I wish, I wish, I wish, I wish...
Psst. Will you help us? Before you turn this page, Close your eyes and wish for us.... Wish us out into the world. Ready? Go!

WISHING WORKED!
WE'RE OUT!
THE WORLD IS
GREAT!
I'VE MADE.
LOTS OF FRIENDS.
HOPE YOU'RE
NOT TOO LONELY!
BACK SOON.

TO YOU!

24

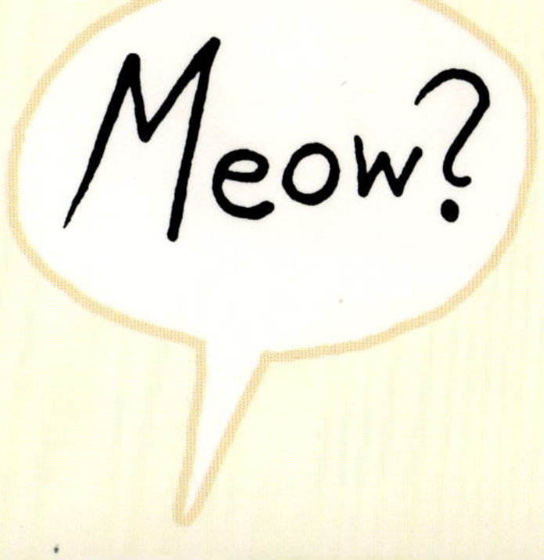
Meow?

Ah,
home sweet
home...

We brought you
a surprise.
Would you like a
surprise?